BLACK CLOUD

Things That Go Bump - Volume IV

© 2014 Daniel Perry

All Rights Reserved

ISBN 13: 978-1497579316

ISBN 10: 1497579317

Things That Go Bump

Series Book 4

Short Story

Black Cloud

For James, like I have always told you,
there will always a way to reinvent yourself.

"Living is subjective, then again so is death."

-Nicholas Dubai-

Books by: Daniel Perry

Non-Fiction

Safe and Sound
(A Family Guide to Self-Defense)

Black Belt Economics

Modern Tournament Production

Children's

The Case of the Missing Shoes

Fiction

The Chimera Alpha Project

Short Stories

Shadows
(Things That Go Bump - Volume 1)

Coven-Rule (Things That Go Bump Volume 2)

Saved by the Bell
(Things That Go Bump - Volume 3)

Black Cloud
(Things That Go Bump - Volume 4)

Trackers (Things That Go Bump - Volume 5)

All characters and information presented in this book are fictional and born from the imagination of the author. Any similarity to anyone living or deceased is pure coincidence and should not be seen as anything other than that

1

Of all the para-beings that exist in this world, vampires have gotten the most bad press. The stories about them, passed from generation to generation have been skewed as well.

Vampires that have been glamourized in writing and in movies and the myths created from such has stuck in the belief systems of the humans. Fact is, vampires are dead in every way you can see it. They have no heartbeat, they do not breath. They are able to sustain themselves through the nutrients received by ingesting live blood. This has to be done at a minimum of every two to three weeks.

One of the largest mistakes that has been made is that vampires bite necks to drink blood. The reality is, they do not have fangs and do not bite. Usually, they will have a sharp fingernail on the first finger and use it to puncture an artery in order to harvest the blood. It has to be consumed while the cells are still alive in order for it to work.

The blood keeps their body working and will absorb for a period of time before they need to feed again. In modern day, they run blood banks and plasma centers so that supply is always readily available and no humans need be harmed. Blood is the way vampires survive and without it they will not be able to sustain.

Daylight is not a problem for vampires, nor is garlic or crosses. Driving a stake through their heart will work to dispatch a vampire only because it drains the blood that is depended on in order to function.

Vampires are incredibly strong and fast. They age at a rate of one year for every ten years that a human does.

They are around for a very long time but contrary to the myths, they do not last forever.

They have also, for whatever reason, been associated with bats. Truth is, there is no comparison to be made. It had proliferated for so long that groups of vampires, even today are sometimes referred to as a cloud, as in "a cloud of bats".

Really, without the knowledge of some of the little tells, you would never know if you were in the presence of a vampire.

This species has been around for centuries. They have had time to amass vast wealth and knowledge that is passed from one generation to the next. They tend to be reclusive in their daily affairs and live extremely private lives.

One thing Hollywood almost got right, is the way they portray these creatures as seductive. Even though there is no truth regarding the bite of a vampire, the mutated parvovirus that creates them is a sexually transmitted disease.

It is believed that the stories about the boogie man were in fact about vampires. There has been one consistent thing in all the time these monsters have been on this earth, they have hated the lycanthropes (werewolves).

The feud has gone on for so long that neither side really remembers why they hate each other so much. For the last few centuries, there has been no blood shed between them. They just simply stay away from one another.

2

Nicholas has been the head of the family for the past two hundred and thirty years. He has personally been responsible for bringing the colony into the technology age.

Through all the time and changes he has seen, there has never been a threat that he has taken to be as serious as the one they are now facing. After discovering that literally all of the other para-being species are involved in this mutiny, he was determined to find out if any of the vampire colony had involvement as well.

Like any good leader, Nicholas has those in the ranking order under him, who he feels can be trusted. They have been instructed to dig as deep as needed. To use whatever means necessary to find out if there is dissention in the colony.

Sirus Norday was a high ranking member of the house, third in line to take over as the leader. He had notified Nicholas that he had uncovered some information that might be useful and had scheduled a meeting with him.

Vampires have very little tolerance and even less patience, so it was very unlikely that Sirus being over thirty minutes late for the meeting, was anything but tragic.

Nicholas walked to his desk in the expansive room that he used for an office. The fireplace flickered red and blue flame and the smell of ancient wood permeated the very walls that surrounded him. This place to the visitor, would appear like a museum. To Nicholas, it was a collection of items he had acquired in his lifetime.

Unknown to all outside of the vampire world, the species had gone high tech. Each member of the colony had been implanted with a small GPS system tracking device so that Nicholas could know their where-a-bouts at any given moment in case of an emergency. This seemed like a good opportunity to utilize the system.

It was easy enough to locate the small orange blip on the computer screen associated with the GPS tracker that was implanted into Sirus. He was currently in a remote area along the Ocoee River. He was not moving and after watching for signs for several minutes, Nicholas determined his body had been rendered inanimate. He really could not say Sirus was dead because of course, vampires are always dead.

The problem was going to be that this area was known to have a large bear population and the body needed to be recovered before an animal dragged it off to another location. One of the ways vampires had stayed hidden for so long was by cleaning up after themselves. It just would not do for human authority to find a vampire body and do something crazy like an autopsy.

Sure, it was easy on television and in the movies. When a vampire is dispatched, they turn to dust with no trace they ever existed. The reality is, a vampire body rots just like any other and decomposes into the earth.

Nicholas summoned a disposal team to go and retrieve the body. Protocol was that vampire bodies were to be cremated immediately. This time was different. Nicholas gave directions that he was to be notified upon their return and he would view the remains prior to disposal.

3

It was not long before the clean-up crew returned with the body. They had taken it to the lower level of the estate where an area was set up complete with a crematorium. He was laid out on a cold stainless steel table and Nicholas had been notified.

Nicholas made quick work of examining the body on the table in front of him. He had long ago lost any emotional contact with anything, grief and mourning had no place in his being.

After checking all of the usual places he began a cavity search. Lucky for him he found what he was looking for under the swollen tongue of the inanimate mass that used to be Sirus. A small flash drive no larger than a fingernail. Nicholas took his prize and motioned for the others to proceed with the fiery destruction of the body.

Back in his den, Nicholas placed the small electronic device into the port on the side of his computer and began to upload the data it contained.

The evidence contained in the files was undisputable. There were photos, notes and transcripts of conversations linking the top two seniors in the colony with the planned uprising. There was information about the number of recruits and even the location of their headquarters located about forty minutes away in Cleveland, Tennessee. All of this would help in planning an offensive.

A name had been given to the group spearheading the uprising. They were calling themselves The League. Jordan Pasqual, who was second in command behind

Nicholas, was in the process of attempting to recruit vampires for The League.

The purpose seemed straight forward enough. This group was tired of hiding in the shadows. They see themselves as superior creatures and want a world where they rule the human race and are allowed to use them as they please. It had taken centuries to get this under control and build a system that allowed the para-beings to coexist. Now they wanted to destroy all the progress in a very short period of time.

The plan was to cut the head off of the snake so to speak and use fear to gain control and compliance of the others. This means that Nicholas, Mary, and Adam were the targets.

Nicholas spent the remainder of the afternoon getting in touch with vampire dens all over the country. He found that most had no idea a situation was brewing giving some hope to the fact that this may be more local and not nationwide or global as he had feared. The other houses even offered and pledged their cooperation and help if need be in the upcoming conflict.

His next call was to Mary, in order to inform her of the new information he had. She picked up the phone on the first ring, "Hello Nicholas." For the longest time, he had believed her ability to know it was him calling had to do with the magic she possessed. That was until he learned about caller ID. The Blood Lord was so embarrassed by this, he decided to embrace technology and learn all he could about this new information era.

"I wanted to make sure you understand that the heads of each para-being unit is being targeted to be eliminated," he told her.

"I understand that perfectly, Nicholas," she chimed. "I have set up a meeting with Adam this afternoon, would you like to come?"

"You know I cannot," he told her. "There may be a time when there is no option, for now, however, I will allow you to act as liaison."

"You know how important this is for all of us, Nicholas. I am willing to talk with Adam by myself, for now. Make no mistake, you do not –ALLOW- me to do anything." She hung up the phone abruptly.

4

Adam sat in the living room of the estate owned by the pack. He stared intently at the fire crackling in the fireplace, popping and sending red embers in all directions. He was worried, as he should be. After all, as the alpha, it was his job to protect the pack at all costs.

He was waiting for a visitor. Mary Martin had wanted to talk with him in regards to the uprising. Hoping she would bring more information to the table to shed light on the situation, he had agreed to meet.

Adam knew this was his responsibility. After all, the thing had been brought to his attention initially due to stray wolf attacks that seemed to be aimed at creating wandering spirits. It was all a little crazy.

A knock on the door alerted Adam his guest had arrived. Mary told him she would be brief. "If you have not been informed, you need to know that all of the para-beings are involved in this." She outlined the ghost and zombie involvement by manipulation. "The fact is Adam, they are planning on controlling by fear after they eliminate you, me and Nicholas."

Adam's eyebrows pushed down hard as he scowled at hearing the vampire's name. "What does that cold bastard have to say about it?"

Mary looked at Adam with a stern expression. "He knows that it will take all of us to bring this to an end. Like you, it seems he still harbors some feelings that you both should be long past."

Adam nodded in response. "Where do you suggest we start?"

Mary related the story of how the zombies were being recruited. She told Adam about how Nicholas had dispatched one of the leaders at the funeral home.

"I know by now the word is out that we are onto them. I think if the wolves would take the fight directly to the zombies, one hard and fast assault would deter them from having any further involvement in the cause."

Adam agreed with this assessment and told her that he would put together a team of hunters to strike tonight.

"Adam, take care of yourself and please let me know when it is done." Mary left the house knowing full well that she had not told him everything she could have. Not yet.

5

Cleveland, Tennessee was a medium sized town with all the charm of a small town. About a quarter of a mile past the west boundary was an old cannery that used to produce pickles. The walls were permeated with the smell of dill and brine and it was the perfect location for The League.

Jordan Pasqual stood in front of a mirror in a back office. It is false that vampires cannot see their reflection. He holds a knife in his right hand. After a quick examination, he slices his left forearm vertically taking care not to sever any of the major vessels that could lead to excessive blood loss. The incision is about three inches long. He needs the space to dig.

With a pair of tweezers Jordan begins to probe deep into his forearm. Past the fatty tissue and muscle, down next to the bone. He never makes a sound or even grimaces as he pulls from the flesh a small chip. Dropping it on the floor he stomps with the heel of his black boot effectively crushing the tracking device. A needle and thread would be needed to repair the arm.

Jordan was always very good at being number two. He had followed the direction Nicholas set for well over a century now. Always wanting more but afraid to defy Nicholas, like a child behaving to avoid parental punishment. Now was going to be his time. Although he had only been able to convince one other vampire to join him so far, two vampires could create a lot of havoc.

He was completely separated from the colony now and with-in the next few days would need to feed. For the first time in too long to remember, Jordan was going to go hunting and it would be for human prey. The thought of it created so much excitement within him that it was nearly impossible to contain.

Eliza Bennett was in the next room and when the vampire appeared with the tools needed, he began to sew up the wound that had been created. It may be just a little bit bitter-sweet that it took such horrific plans to bring a wolf and vampire together as allies. Good or bad, there is a historical element to it.

6

Nicholas sat at his computer. It was time to locate Jordan and attempt to stop this madness. When he pulled up the map with all of the little yellow dot indicators that showed the global position of every member of the colony, Jordan's tracker was not there. He rebooted with the same result. It could only be that the tracker had been deactivated somehow.

Nicholas slammed his fist hard on the table. The force of the blow slit the three inch thick oak as if it were thin balsa. "This would not do," he thought. Not at all.

The evening brought with it the kind of wind that blows through your skin and chills your soul. Nicholas paid no attention as he walked to the witch's little shop on the square. His mind was preoccupied with the fact that something had to happen and it needed to be sooner rather than later. He knew Mary had a meeting with Adam earlier. Although there was so much bad blood between them, he was curious as to what had been said.

Mary met him at the door as if she knew he was walking up. "Nicholas," she said. "I am glad you are here. We have a lot to talk about."

Nicholas went inside the shop with her. The smell of sandalwood incense was overpowering. They sat on tall stools at the counter and Mary excused herself for just a minute to put on a pot of tea. This would be a regular, everyday tea. She knew all too well that magic did not work on a vampire.

After serving the tea in small blue and white porcelain cups with matching saucers, she sat next to the head of the vampires to tell him what she knew so far.

After she explained that the wolf pack was one hundred percent with them and the plan to attack the zombies to increase the fear already spreading among them, she quieted so that Nicholas could relay any news he may have about the situation.

Nicholas told of his findings and the fact that recruiting vampires for their cause was going to be very difficult for The League. "Unfortunately, one or two vampires on their team can be quite a threat," he added.

"I have an idea that may help us to obtain an advantage," Mary told him. "Since the coven polices the world of spirits, I have been in touch with one in particular that wants to help in any way he can. He was taken from this world by a stray wolf and is looking for a little bit of payback, I think. Even more Nicholas, there are spirits that reside in the courthouse next door that my gut tells me we need to talk to. The problem is, when they are there at night, the building is closed and locked to the public."

Nicholas put his hand up to his chin, cupping it in his fist as if deep in thought. "I believe I can solve that problem." His half smile was the first sign he had ever given her that he had any emotions at all.

7

The sun had already set and now was as good a time as any for the pair to make a house call at the courthouse. Mary grabbed a shawl to help fight against the cold air and locked the shop door behind them.

The building was old so Nicholas had no trouble using the unnatural strength he possessed to push on the door until the latch that held it, moaned and began to bend, giving way and allowing them entrance.

The foyer was immense and beautiful in design with winding stairs that led towards a huge dome ceiling. The floors, as well as the staircase, were laid with marble that seemed to glow in the dim florescent lighting, due to the maintenance buffing them on a daily basis.

Mary stood in the center of the large room and began to speak. "It is important the spirits of this building make themselves known. There is a storm brewing that affects us all and your help may be needed to help quell it. We mean you no harm and no punishments are due upon you. Present yourselves now for all our sakes."

Mary had known about two spirits that haunted this building. She could feel them. She also knew they were good souls. It surprised her when six appeared in the great room. Four female and two male, not that it made any difference in that world.

"Thank you," she said out loud. "At some point, I would like to get to know each of you better. For now, we are facing a crisis and I am asking for your help. There is a group of rogue para-beings attempting to destroy everything we have put in place to live peacefully with the humans. They are strong, but we believe their numbers are low. We have located their headquarters and need information to help with a counter to their plans. I am hoping that is where you will come in. I have a spirit friend who would be willing to lead you, as a group, in order for you to use your special set of skills. I am asking for all of our sakes and for the sake of mankind, will you help?"

As quick as they appeared, the ghosts faded away leaving Mary and Nicholas standing to stare at each other. It was only a few minutes before four were back. One appeared directly in front of Mary and began to speak. "My name is Colton McGret. We have talked it over and the four of us would like to help. The other two were pretty young when they died and spook easily. They are afraid of encountering witches and have never left this building, even when they could. So if you are willing to respect that and leave the kids alone, you have us. Just tell us what to do."

Mary looked at the spirit and smiled. "We are glad to have you. The friend I spoke of is Kevin Hall. He was killed by a wolf as part of their plot. I will send him to you and he will explain everything. Thank you again." With that, the ghosts once again vanished. Nicholas and Mary exited the building and returned to the potion shop.

"I hope you know what you are doing, my dear," Nicholas said.

"I believe it will give us an advantage. There is much to do and we do not even know yet what our timeline is. So for now, goodnight, Nicholas. I will let you know when I know more."

8

Jordan was out prowling the streets of Cleveland. Hunting for food was something he had never had to do but seemed to have a keen instinct for. He could not help thinking to himself that this is how it was supposed to be: Predator and prey.

The first finger of his right hand had an inch and a half sharpened nail. This would be his weapon. It had to be done tonight. Any longer and he could be too weak to hunt. He wasn't ready to think any of his league members would do anything except allow him to expire.

BLACK CLOUD

A woman about twenty two years old had parked her car and started down the trail. This city was fantastic. There were public trails all over town and the public had grown secure in their safety, even at night.

She placed the ear buds in both ears and turned the music up. No way for her to hear another approaching. This had to be perfect. How could it be so easy?

As soon as she had cleared most of the light, he struck, quickly from the shadows that concealed him. The left hand over the mouth to prevent the scream from escaping and the weapon driving into the soft flesh on the right side of her neck, punching a hole directly into the carotid artery.

The amount of pressure behind the blood spray startled him at first. Quickly overtaken by a hunger that cannot be defined, he began to feed. This warm blood was possibly the best feeling he had had since being turned. It was the salty taste as it slid down his throat and the energy it gave him almost immediately.

More than that, he was enjoying himself. Holding this person in a tight grip, he felt the life being drained from the body. Yes, he thought, I win.

THE CHIMERA ALPHA PROJECT

Don't miss the first full length novel by:

Daniel Perry

Available April 2014

Made in the USA
Coppell, TX
27 August 2021